SONOMA STATE UNIVERSITY RUBEN SALAZAR LIBRARY

WITHDRAWN

P9-BHT-366

FAIR-WEATHER FRIENDS

Text by Jack Gantos Art by Nicole Rubel

Houghton Mifflin Company Boston 1977

TO THE TWINS

Library of Congress Cataloging in Publication Data

Gantos, Jack.
    Fair-weather friends.

    SUMMARY: Though best friends, Maggie and
Chester must separate as she prefers to live
in the North and he, the South.
    [1. Friendship--Fiction] I. Rubel, Nicole,
joint author. II. Title.
PZ7.G15334Fai   [E]   76-62500
ISBN 0-395-25156-7

Copyright © 1977 by John B. Gantos Jr.
Copyright © 1977 by Leslie Rubel
All rights reserved. No part of this work may
be reproduced or transmitted in any form by any
means, electronic or mechanical, including
photocopying and recording, or by any information
storage or retrieval system, without permission
in writing from the publisher.
Printed in the United States of America
H 10 9 8 7 6 5 4 3 2 1

Maggie and Chester are best friends. They
live very far up in the freezing North. All year
long the ground is covered with snow and ice.

Chester hates the North. He is always grumpy.
The snow and icicles stick to his whiskers.
And the cold air makes his nose turn purple.

Maggie loves the North. Her doors and windows
are always open. Her favorite sport is throwing
snowballs. And she likes to ice-skate too.

One day Chester could no longer stand the cold.
"If I spend another day up North I'll bite someone!"
he growled.

Maggie wished Chester could be happier. "Perhaps
a vacation in the South will cheer you up," she
suggested.

"A great idea!" shouted Chester. "Will you
join me?" he asked.

"Of course I will," Maggie replied. "I'm your
best friend."

They decided to leave that evening. Chester
got his rowboat and Maggie made some sandwiches.

"Let's hurry up!" Chester snapped. "My feet
are freezing."

"Bon Voyage!" their friends hollered.

"So long!" yelled Maggie and Chester. Then
Chester began to row and Maggie steered for the
South.

The first night out they ran into a terrible storm. Huge waves kept filling the rowboat with water.

"I think I'm getting seasick," moaned Maggie. "Let's not go South."

"Please, don't get sick now," pleaded Chester. "If you stop bailing we'll sink."

Maggie knew Chester had his heart set on reaching the South. She felt awful but she kept on bailing. And before long the storm began to calm.

The next morning Maggie went swimming. "Jump in, the water's fine!" she shouted to Chester.

Without thinking Chester dove head first into the water. He came up screaming. "Help! Help! I'm turning into an iceberg."

"What's wrong with you?" asked Maggie. She thought the water was very refreshing.

But Chester couldn't answer. He was so cold he thought his teeth would fall out.

Rowing made them very hungry and soon they had eaten all their sandwiches. Chester began to fish and hooked a fat tuna. But each time he pulled a fish out of the water a pelican swooped down and ate it.

"Crazy birds!" he hollered at them. Chester was very upset.

"This would never happen in the North," said Maggie.

"This won't happen in the South either," said Chester. "There will be enough bananas and coconuts for both of us."

After a few more days they finally landed on
a warm and sandy beach. Chester was very excited.

"Paradise!" he shouted.

But Maggie was feeling awful. "This sun
makes me dizzy," she moaned. "And I can hardly
breathe. This air is hotter than a furnace."

Chester wanted to try everything. That night
he talked Maggie into going calypso dancing. Chester
tapped his feet and snapped his fingers.

"This is wonderful!" he yelled. "I'm having
the best time of my life."

But Maggie became very grumpy. "This heat has
ruined my fur," she snarled. "If I dance another
minute I'll melt."

In the morning Chester insisted that they explore the tropical jungle.

"Just look at the exotic birds and plants," he exclaimed.

"The bugs are biting me," cried Maggie. "I don't enjoy being eaten alive in your tropical paradise." She felt miserable.

The next day Maggie was feeling worse.

"I'm sorry, Chester," she said. "I have to leave the South. I have a terrible sunburn. There are too many bugs. And this heat will soon make me mad enough to bite even you!"

"I'm sorry too," said Chester. "As much as I like you I just can't stand the North. I will have to stay in the South. This is where I am happy."

It was a very sad moment when the two friends parted.

"It's too bad we can't be happy in the same place," said Chester.

"But we'll always be friends," remarked Maggie.

"I hope the snow makes you cheerful," Chester said sincerely.

"And I hope the heat always keeps you smiling," said Maggie.

Then they kissed goodbye and Maggie set sail for the North.

Maggie had a safe voyage home.
Soon she was riding a toboggan with some
friends. She loved the icy breezes and the feel
of snow on her paws. She missed Chester but the
North was the only home for her.

Chester was lonely without Maggie. But
before long he met some new friends who
taught him how to surf. He was very glad not to
have icicles on his ears all the time. He loved
the water at the beach and the hot sun on
his nose. The South was the best place for him.

So Maggie enjoys the North.

And Chester is never grumpy in the South.

But they always take time to think of

each other.

They exchange lots of postcards and letters.

Dear Chester,
I miss you. I
built A SNOWMAN
To Look just like
you. The weather
is FINE. Write
soon.
xx Maggie xx

P.S. Visit Me Soon

LODGE IN THE
SNOWY MOUNTAINS

Dear Maggie,
I've been eatting
a lot of coconuts
I miss you but I
don't miss the
blizzards. I like
exploring the jungle
Write Soon. xx
chester

P.S. Visit me soon

A TIDAL WAVE

And they visit just as often as they can.